CEARBHALL AND FEARBHLAIDH

DOLMEN TEXTS 7

THE ROMANCE OF CEARBHALL AND FEARBHLAIDH TRANSLATED BY JAMES E. DOAN FROM THE IRISH

THE DOLMEN PRESS, MOUNTRATH, IRELAND
NORTH AMERICA: HUMANITIES PRESS INC.

DOLMEN TEXTS

Set in Palatino type by Redsetter Limited, Dublin
Printed in Great Britain by Billing & Sons Ltd., Worcester

The Dolmen Press Limited, Mountrath, Portlaoise, Ireland.

North America: Humanities Press Inc., Atlantic Highlands,
New Jersey 07716.

Designed by Liam Miller
Title vignette drawn by Deirdre Cullen

First published 1985

British Library Cataloguing in Publication Data
    The Romance of Cearbhall and Fearbhlaidh——
    (Dolmen texts; 7).
        I. Doan, James E.
        891.6'234   PR8821

891.62
R758-T

ISBN 0 85105 409 9 The Dolmen Press

86-3270

To my grandmother
for all her love and support.

CONTENTS

FOREWORD

THE INITIAL IMPETUS for this translation came from a Modern Irish seminar conducted by Professor Patrick K. Ford at U.C.L.A. in the winter of 1976, in which we read one of the folktales dealing with Cearbhall Ó Dálaigh, published in *Béaloideas* 3 (1931). Two years later, while working on my Ph.D. in Folklore and Celtic Studies at Harvard University, my interest in Cearbhall was again sparked when I began to conduct research on another Ó Dálaigh, Muireadhach Albanach, in a course given by Professor Charles Dunn during the spring of 1978. That summer, while studying at the Dublin Institute for Advanced Studies, I became intrigued by the question of the identity of the poet, or poets, named Cearbhall Ó Dálaigh, which led ultimately to my writing a Ph.D. dissertation on this subject entitled, 'Cearbhall Ó Dálaigh: An Irish Poet in Romance and Oral Tradition' (Diss. Harvard University, 1981). The present translation forms part of one chapter of that dissertation.

I cannot begin to name everyone who has given me assistance in preparing this translation. However, I would particularly like to thank Professor John Armstrong of Harvard University who first read the Irish text of the romance with me during the autumn of 1978. In addition, I would like to thank my colleagues, Cornelius Buttimer and Michele Carly, who attended our meetings and offered many helpful suggestions concerning the translation, several of which are incorporated here. I would also like to thank Tomás Ó Cathasaigh of University College, Dublin, who offered many invaluable insights into the poetry contained in the romance. Finally, I would like to thank Professors Charles Dunn and John Kelleher

[7]

who read this translation and provided numerous stylistic suggestions which I have also included. Of course, I take full responsibility for the translation and any errors which may occur therein.

James E. Doan

INTRODUCTION

I THE MANUSCRIPT TRADITION

THE ROMANCE OF CEARBHALL AND FEARBH-
LAIDH was probably composed during the second
half of the fifteenth, or first half of the sixteenth century, possibly by an Ó Dálaigh poet ca. 1450[1] The tale
is found in twenty manuscripts, dating from the early
1600's to the 1840's, as follows:

Ulster

A[1] Franciscan Library, Killiney, A 25, written ca. 1608-28.
H[1] TCD H.4.25, written ca. 1630-40.
P[1] RIA 24 P 12, written before 1648.
R[1] Rossmore, Co. Monaghan, 2, written in 1712.
G[1] NLI G 130, written 1725-27.
G[2] NLI G 144, written in 1767.
H[2] TCD H.6.8, written in 1777 by Labhras Ó Tárann.
B[1] RIA 24 . 13, written in 1780 by Seaghán Gaillidhe.
P[3] RIA 24 P 21, written in the eighteenth or nineteenth
       century.
P[4] RIA 24 P 31, written before 1816 by Peadar Úa Dálaigh.
B[2] RIA 3 B 39, written in 1847 by Peadar Úa Gealacáin.
B[3] Belfast Library 15, written in 1849 by Aodh Mac
       Domhnaill.

Munster

M[1] RIA 23 M 25, written in 1684 by Eóghan Ó Caoimh,
       Co. Cork.
K[1] RIA 23 K 7, written in 1700 by Domhnall Mac
       Donnchadha.
P[2] RIA 24 P 6, written in 1768 by Ríghrí Mac Raghnaill,
       Co. Cork.
E[1] RIA 23 E 16, written in 1797 by Mícheal Óg Ó Longáin,
       Co. Cork.

M²ˈMaynooth M 19, written in 1817 by Pól Ó Longáin, Co. Cork.
E² RIA E V 2, written in 1819-20 by Pól Ó Longáin.
D¹ RIA 23 D 26, written before 1825 by Cathal Úa Tuacoidh, Tipperary.
A² RIA 24 A 23, written ca. 1843 by an Ó Longáin.

The earliest surviving Ulster manuscripts, A¹, H¹ and P¹, are fairly close to one another, which suggests that they are based on a common exemplar, perhaps a copy made in Ulster during the sixteenth century. H¹ has been expanded and modernized to a certain extent, undoubtedly because the scribe had a difficult time copying the manuscript which was before him.² None of these manuscripts gives a title to the romance, although they do provide an end title: *bas Cerbaill 7 Farblaidhe* ('the death of C. and F.') in A¹, *eachtra 7 bas Cerbaill Uí Dhálaigh 7 Farbhlaidhe inghine riogh Alban* ('the adventure and death of C. Ó D. and F., daughter of the king of Scotland') in H¹, and *imteacht 7 bas Cherbhaill 7 Fharbhluidhe* ('the adventure and death of C. and F.') in P¹.

K¹, written in 1700, was the first manuscript to give the title *Tochmharc Fhearbhlaidhe* ('The Wooing of F.') to the romance. All of the subsequent Munster manuscripts adopted that title, although only one of the Ulster manuscripts did (B¹). Most of them followed the earlier Ulster manuscripts in providing only an end title, although P³ has the title *Beatha Chearbhaill Uí Dhálaigh* ('The Life of C. Ó D.') pencilled in by a later hand. B³ has that title included in the text, and B², which is based on a copy of P³, has the title *Pósadh Cearbhaill Uí Dhálaigh* ('The Marriage of C. Ó D.').

Regarding the spelling of the heroine's name, the earlier manuscripts generally have Farbhlaidh or Farbhladh, rather than Fearbhlaidh, although this became the established convention in the eighteenth century. To avoid confusion I have adopted this spelling consistently. The name itself is apparently based on the OIr. *Forbflaith*, a compound of *for* 'over' *flaith* 'rule', an element found in other royal women's names, such as Gormfhlaith.[2]

Eoghan Ó Neachtain based his edition of the tale, which appeared in *Ériu* 4 (1910), 47-67, primarily on the version found in P[1]. Paul Walsh based his edition in *Irisleabhar Muighe Nuadhat* (1928), 26-45, on the versions found in A[1] and H[1]. Among the various titles and end titles of the tale mentioned above, *Bás Chearbhaill 7 Fhearbhlaidhe* ('The Death of Cearbhall and Fearbhlaidh') is the oldest and best attested, so that I shall henceforth refer to the romance by that title, abbreviated as *BCF*. The chapter numbers refer to those found in the translation, which correspond to those found in both Ó Neachtain's and Walsh's editions.

II THE COMPOSITION OF THE ROMANCE

Although the romance ends with the tragic death of the two lovers, it also includes several other themes dealing with love (*searc*) which undoubtedly suggested the various titles. These themes include the following:

1) the unsuccessful wooing (*tochmharc*) of Fearbhlaidh by the kings and lords of Western Europe (Ch. 1). Cearbhall also attempts to woo her, but he is caught and sentenced to death by her father, Séamas (Ch. 32-37).
2) the dream vision (*aisling*) in which Fearbhlaidh first sees Cearbhall and falls in love with him (Ch. 5).
3) the magical shape-shifting by which Duibhghil,

Fearbhlaidh's nurse (Ch. 8-10), and then both women (Ch. 16), travel from Scotland to Ireland and back again in the form of doves. Later, they come to Ireland in the form of swans (Ch. 54).

4) the Otherworld journey (*eachtra*, 'adventure'), here presented as Fearbhlaidh's visit to Cearbhall in the burren of Co. Clare (Ch. 16-24).

5) the wasting sickness (*searg*) which Cearbhall suffers after Fearbhlaidh returns to Scotland, and which can only be cured by a stone of healing sent by her (Ch. 24-27). Later in the story, the women in Fearbhlaidh's retinue, and the men in Cearbhall's, suffer a wasting sickness caused from grief at the absence of their respective spouses in the other group (Ch. 44).

6) the sleeping-music (*suantraí*) which causes everyone to fall asleep except the two lovers and Duibhghil (Ch. 32-34).

7) Fearbhlaidh's madness (*gealtacht*) another form of love sickness, which occurs when Cearbhall is placed in prison and sentenced to death by her father (Ch. 37), and Cearbhall's madness after he escapes from the prison in Scotland and returns to Ireland (Ch. 44).

8) In addition to the *searg* and *gealtacht*, Cearbhall suffers a third type of love sickness when he takes a drink of forgetfulness (*deoch dhearmaid*), forgets about Fearbhlaidh, marries another woman named Ailbhe, and then despairs when he remembers Fearbhlaidh and realizes what he has done (Ch. 45-53). While this could be interpreted as a type of *gealtacht*, it is closer in style to the *folie of Tristan*) after he marries Yseut aux Blanches Mains in Brittany, then despairs when he recalls Yseut in Cornwall, or Yvain's madness when he forgets to return to his wife Laudine

[12]

after a year's absence until he is reminded by her maid Lunete, by which time it is too late.

9) finally, the falsely-reported death of Cearbhall which leads first to Fearbhlaidh's death, and then to Cearbhall's when he learns that she has died (Ch. 59-63). Although this theme is found in the early Irish tale of Baile and Ailinn (*Scél Baili Binnbérlaig*), it is more characteristic of Continental and British romance and tragedy, e.g., Tristan and Yseut, or Romeo and Juliet.

It is clear that the author of *BCF* was well-versed in the traditional Irish sagas and romances which formed the basis for many of the fifteenth- and sixteenth-century romances. The *tochmharc* theme was possibly suggested by his knowledge of 'The Wooing of Étaín' daughter of Étar, who is the reincarnation of the 'goddess' Étaín Eochraide, by her former lover, the 'god' Midir.

In 'The Wooing of Étaín,' Midir tricks Étaín's husband, Eochaid Airem, king of Ireland, into giving her to him by means of a game of *fidhcheall* (OIr. *fidchell*, a board game, usually translated as 'chess'). The two lovers escape from the palace of Eochaid at Tara in the form of two swans, but they are pursued to the *sídhe* ('fairy mounds') by Eochaid and the men of Ireland. After the latter destroy two of the *sídhe*, Eochaid is told to choose his own wife from among the assembled Otherworld women, but he chooses his own daughter by mistake. In some versions of the story, when Eochaid realizes that he has been deceived, he returns to the fairy mound, and this time Étaín makes herself known to him, after which he bears her away to Tara. In the conclusion to the story, Eochaid is slain by Mormael, king of the Fir Chúl, and by Sigmall, Midir's grandson. They also burn Eochaid's stronghold and bring his head to Síd Nennta in Meath, 'in vengeance for the honor of Midir'.[3]

In 'The Destruction of Da Derga's Hostel,' the sequel to 'The Wooing of Étaín', Étaín's daughter by Eochaid is also named Étaín. In 'The Wooing,' this girl bears a daughter to her own father, although in 'The Destruction' this has been censored, so that she bears a child to her husband, 'Cormac, king of Ulster,' instead. In both tales, this child is abandoned at birth, but rescued by a herdsman who raises her, hence her name: Mes Buachalla ('The Herdsman's Fosterling'). She in turn marries Eterscél, king of Ireland. Before the marriage, however, she is visited by an Otherworld being who comes to her in the form of a bird. He sheds his birdskin and sleeps with her, telling her that she will bear a son who must not kill birds. This son is Conaire Mór, who becomes king of Ireland after Eterscél's death.

Conaire Mór is eventually slain at Da Derga's Hostel. His death is structurally parallel to that of his grandfather (also his great-grandfather), Eochaid Airem, since he too is beheaded and the hostel destroyed. On the other hand, Conaire's death comes about because of *geasa* (taboos), including the injunction not to kill birds which had been imposed upon him by his father. According to one version of 'The Wooing,' the people of the Otherworld caused Conaire to break his *geasa*, knowing that this would cause his death, because Eochaid had destroyed the *sídhe* and taken away Étaín by force.[4] Thus, according to this account, Étaín would be ultimately responsible for the death of both Eochaid Airem and Conaire Mór, since both resulted at least indirectly from her elopement with Midir, Eochaid's pursuit of them, and the destruction of the two *sídhe*.

In *BCF* Séamas mac Turcaill, Fearbhlaidh's father, is said to be from the race of Cairbre Rioghfhada son of Conaire (Ch. 1), the ancestor of the Dál Riada from whom the Scottish kings claimed descent. According to the genealogies, this Cairbre was either the son of Conaire Mór or his descendant to the seventh generation.[5] In either case he was also a descendant of Étaín.

In Chapter 5 of *BCF* Fearbhlaidh admits to her father that she has fallen in love with a man who appeared to her in a vision. Séamas warns her against heeding an Otherworld phantom (*siabhradh sídhe*), and then bemoans the legacy of her ancestress,

> Étaín daughter of Eochraidh, the wife of Eochaid Airem, and the other Étaín who was her daughter, and moreover Mes Buachalla, daughter of Eochaid, the mother of Conaire son of Eterscél (Ch. 6).

Presumably, Séamas fears that history will repeat itself. Two women in the family, namely Étaín and Mes Buachalla, had previously enjoyed sexual contact with men from the Otherworld, with disastrous results, and Fearbhlaidh seems to be on the same course.

It is interesting to note that the author of *BCF*, or else the redactor of the sixteenth-century version, was familiar with a form of 'The Wooing of Étaín' in which Étaín's daughter was also named Étaín, as in 'The Destruction of Da Derga's Hostel,' rather than Ésa as in the older versions.[6] He seems to have been relying on 'The Wooing' rather than 'The Destruction' for the familial relationships, since he makes Étaín I the wife of Eochaid Airem, rather than of Eochaid Feidlech as in 'The Destruction,' and Mes Buachalla the daughter of Eochaid, rather than of 'Cormac'. On the other hand, he has substituted a form of Étaín's epithet,

Eochraide ('horse-riding' or 'swift'), for the name of her father, originally Étar.

Séamas also states that he regrets that the nature of Fearbhlaidh's kinswoman, Baillgheal daughter of Mugh Lámha, is coming through her. According to one genealogy, this Baillgheal was a wife of Conn Céadchathach who was carried off by Forgna, king of Connacht, possibly to his fairy mound, since he was said to have been brought to Síd Rionduilbh in Connacht after the battle of Magh Mucramha, 'and has been there ever since.'[7] This Baillgheal was presumably the sister of Conaire mac Mogha Lámha, the father of Cairbre Rioghfhada in some genealogies, who is also given as the son-in-law of Conn Céadchathach, whom he succeeded in the kingship of Ireland.[8] Here follows a genealogy showing the relationships between the characters mentioned in *BCF* and the relevant personages from the genealogical and romance traditions.

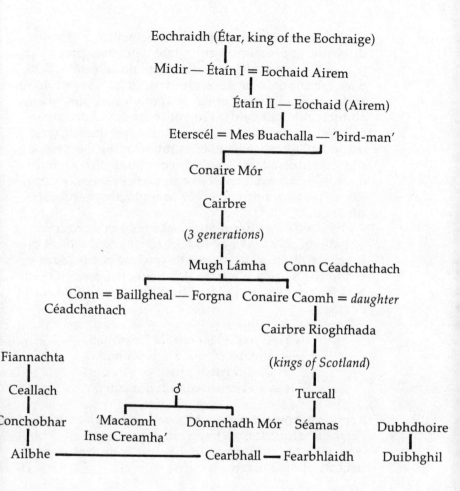

= indicates marriage
— indicates illicit relationship

Figure 1. A Genealogy Showing the Relationships between the Characters in *Bás Chearbhaill 7 Fhearbhlaidhe* and Relevant Personages from the Genealogical and Romance Traditions.

The tradition of Baillgheal's elopement with Forgna does not appear until quite late, and was probably part of the oral tradition with which the author of BCF was familiar. It is possibly a doublet for Midir's abduction of Étaín, since in both cases the lover abducts the wife of the king of Ireland and presumably takes her to his fairy mound. In BCF the author is using Baillgheal as another example of the dangerous consequences of Otherworld seductions, although we do not know what those consequences were, except that Séamas implies that they brought about Ireland's ruin (Ch. 6).

One finds another reference to Forgna's seduction of Baillgheal, as well as to Cearbhall's 'seduction' of Fearbhlaidh, in a late sixteenth-century poem addressed to the harpist Nioclás Dall. Using the conceit that Nioclás's music must come from the fairy world, the poet says:

> Nó isé an ceól lér chealg Cearbhall
> Fearbhlaidh fhéta, aisdiormhall,
> ó sheangAlbain na n-eas tte,
> teas go beannardaibh Bhoirne.

(Or it is the music by which Cearbhall beguiled gentle Fearbhlaidh of the stately gait, from beautiful Scotland with its pretty waterfalls, south to the peaked heights of the Burren.)

> Nó isé so an síansa síthe
> lér chealg *Forgna* foiltfhíthe
> Baillghil, do bhrígh na seanma,
> ó rígh ainghidh éactTeamhra.

(Or this is the fairy music by which Forgna with the plaited hair enticed Billgheal through its playing from the wicked king of deed-famed Tara.)[9]

Regarding *BCF*, the scribes of H¹ and P¹ correctly retained the tradition of Baillgheal as daughter of Mugh Lámha ('The Slave of the Hand'), although the scribe of A¹ omitted the woman's name and changed the father's name to Mugh Lámhfhada ('of the Long Hand'), the epithet usually associated with the god Lugh. Elsewhere in *BCF*, the author uses Lugh's soubriquet, *an t-Ioldánach* ('having many skills') for Cearbhall, since he both entertains and instructs the company while playing his harp (Ch. 12).

The author of *BCF* may have also been familiar with 'The Wooing of Emer' in which Lugh's son, Cú Chulainn, woos Emer, the daughter of Forgall Manach. In one episode of this tale, Cú, who has returned to Ireland from Scotland after being trained in arms by the female warrior Scathach, comes to the shore of Loch Cuan (Strangford Lough), sees two birds, and shoots one of them with a stone from his sling. The birds are transformed into two women, Derbforgaill and her handmaid. Derbforgaill, who has been wounded, tells Cú that she has come to meet him. He sucks the stone out of her, but then tells her that he cannot marry her because he has sucked some of her blood as well. Instead he gives her to his companion, Lugaid Reo nDerg. After this, Cú carries Emer off from her father's fortress, leaving him and hundreds of his men dead.[10]

Another version of this is found in 'The Death of Derbforgaill,' in which the two women come to the lough in the form of swans, and Cú throws a stone which passes between Derbforgaill's wings into her breast. In 'The Sick-Bed of Cú Chulainn,' Fand and her sister, Lí Ban, come from the *síodh* to the Plain of Muirtheimne as two birds, and Cú throws a spear which passes through the wing of one of them.[11]

In *BCF* Fearbhlaidh and Duibhghil come to the

River Suck in the form of swans, and a herdsman throws a stone which breaks the wing of one of them. Cearbhall finds the wounded swan and kills the herdsman. Then, both swans change into their own forms, and we see that Duibhghil's left arm is broken (Ch. 54-56). This episode was probably imitated from 'The Death of Derbforgaill,' rather than 'The Wooing of Emer' or 'The Sick-Bed of Cú Chulainn,' since in both 'The Death' and BCF the women appear in the form of swans (géise), and one of them is wounded either 'between the wings' as in 'The Death,' or the wing itself is broken as in BCF.

Nevertheless, one finds other similarities between 'The Wooing of Emer' and BCF, suggesting a possible connection. In both, the woman's father opposes the courtship. Also, the hero travels to Scotland and back again. Scotland is often treated as an Otherworld place of magic and adventure, both in early tales such as 'The Wooing' and in the later romances. In BCF Fearbhlaidh, as well as Duibhghil, has certain Otherworld qualities, since she is able to transform herself from a swan into mortal shape (Ch. 56), as well as assist Duibhghil in making a magical ship to take them back to Scotland (Ch. 58).

In 'The Death of Derbforgaill' we are told that Derbforgaill had set her love on Cú Chulainn 'because of the great stories told of him' (ara urscélaib).[12] This is a conventional reason to explain why a woman falls in love with a certain man in early Irish tales. One finds it, for example, in relation to Findabair and Fróech in 'The Cattle-Raid of Fróech',[13] and with regard to Diarmaid mac Aeda Sláne's daughter and Cano ion 'The Tidings of Cano son of Gartnán.'[14] In the latter work we are told that Créd daughter of Gúaire had loved Cano even before he came from Scotland.[15] These are all examples of grádh éagmaise, 'the love of one who is

[20]

absent,' or the love of one who is known only through his reputation.[16] In Provencal tradition one finds a parallel in the story of the troubadour, Jaufré Rudel, who fell 'in love with the Countess of Tripoli for the good that he heard tell of her from the pilgrims that came from Antioch.'[17]

Another form of *grádh éagmaise* is the *aisling* (dream vision) in which a man sees a beautiful woman in his sleep, falls in love with her and searches throughout the world until he finds her. This is an ancient theme in Celtic literature since it forms the basis not only for the Old Irish *Aislinge Óenguso* ('The Dream of Óengus') but also the Middle Welsh *Breuddwyd Macsen Wledig* ('The Dream of Macsen Wledig'), found in *The Mabinogion*.[18]

In 'The Dream of Óengus,' the god Óengus (Mac ind Óc) dreams that a beautiful woman comes to visit him every night for a year playing on her lyre (*timpán*). He falls into a wasting sickness (*serg*) so that he cannot eat. He tells no one the cause of his illness, but finally the physician Fingen diagnoses it as *serc écmaise* ('love in absence'). Óengus's mother, the goddess Boand, is sent for, and after a year during which the object of his desire is still not found, they send for his father, the Dagda. Boand tells the Dagda that their son is wasting away (*i siurg*, dat. of *serg*), because he has fallen in love in absence, with a possible pun on *serg* and *serc*.[19]

Fingen then tells them to send for Bodb, the king of the *sídhe* in Munster, who asks for a year's respite to find the girl. They return to Bodb's house at the end of a year, and he tells them that he has found her on the shore of Loch Bél Dragon. They bring Óengus to the shore of the lake, and he recognizes her among her one hundred fifty companions. Bodb tells them that she is Caer Ibhormheith from Síd Uamhain in Connacht.

[21]

The Dagda then goes to Connacht to ask Ailill and Medb for the girl. They reply that they have no power over her, so Ailill's steward goes to the girl's father, Ethal Anbuail, to ask him. When he refuses to give the girl, Ailill attacks and captures him. Ethal says that he has no power over her, but that she alternates between human and avian shape every other year. He also tells them that she will be at Loch Bél Dragon the following Samhain (Nov. 1), in the shape of a bird with one hundred fifty swans around her.

Óengus comes to the lake at Samhain and sees the swans on the lake with silver chains connecting them. Óengus calls for Caer, and she answers that she will come with him if he promises that she may return to the lake. He throws his arm around her and they encircle the lake three times in the form of two swans. After this they return to Bruig Maic in Óig (Newgrange) in the form of two white birds, and sing together so that they put the people to sleep for three days and nights. The girl remains with him after that.

Several elements of the *aisling* theme are found in both 'The Dream of Óengus' and in *BCF*, although in the latter the roles are reversed, since the 'Otherworld' visitor is a man (Ch. 5). First of all, Cearbhall appeared to Fearbhlaidh while she was sleeping, playing his harp (*cruit*), in the same way that Caer appeared to Óengus playing the *timpán*. Next, Fearbhlaidh is so affected that she cannot set her eye on any other man (Ch. 1). After her confrontation with her father (Ch. 6-7), she tells her nurse, Duibhghil, who comforts her by saying that she will obtain news of the man within a year, in the same way that Bodb offers to find out about Óengus's beloved within a year. Duibhghil finds Cearbhall playing to his three times fifty (150) companions (Ch. 10-11), as Óengus first sees Caer with three times fifty girls beside the lake. Duibhghil returns to Fearbhlaidh to tell her the news and both women come in the form of doves to visit Cearbhall (Ch. 16). Compare this with Óengus's visit to Caer on Samhain, although in this case the lover is in human form and the beloved in the shape of a bird. Fearbhlaidh remains with Cearbhall for three days and nights (Ch. 22), as Óengus brings Caer to Newgrange (an Otherworld *síodh*) for three days and nights, the conventional period for a stay in the Otherworld.

Clearly, Fearbhlaidh's visit to Cearbhall in the Burren is to be interpreted as a rationalized version of the Otherworld journey (*eachtra*). As Proinsias MacCana states, concerning the geography of this romance:

> The setting is superficially terrestrial, but, as with many of the later romances in Irish, no boundary is set between the natural and the supernatural and most, if not all, the events appear to take place in the Otherworld of Irish storytelling.[20]

As MacCana also suggests, the author of *BCF* indicates this as an Otherworld visit with 'a touch of flippancy' and 'a tongue-in-cheek romanticism.' After Fearbhlaidh reveals her true form, Cearbhall falls in love with her, and after Duibhghil tactfully exits,

> Cearbhall pulled Fearbhlaidh towards him over the side of the flockbed, and he put his hands around her neck and kissed her passionately. They were like that for three days and nights without food or drink, without sleeping or resting, and without sin or blame (Ch. 22).

This view of the Otherworld as a place of innocence or, as stated in 'The Wooing of Étaín,' a place where there will be 'conception without sin, without lust,' is very much within the Irish tradition.[21]

Further evidence that the author of *BCF* intended this as a visit to the Otherworld is provided by Duibhghil's statement when she returns on the third day that, although it has seemed like only three days to Fearbhlaidh, it has been much longer (Ch. 23), another feature of the Otherworld. In addition, when the two women return to Scotland, we are told: 'It had been heard in all of Europe that Fearbhlaidh and her nurse were in the fairy mounds (*a síodhaibh*), so that people fainted from joy at finding them' (Ch. 24).

Another motif in 'The Dream of Óengus' has a parallel in *BCF*, namely the sleeping-music which Cearbhall plays at Séamas's court (Ch. 32-34), like the 'choral song' which Óengus and Caer sing in Newgrange to put everyone to sleep. On the other hand, this theme of the feast where everyone falls asleep except the two lovers is also found in 'The Tidings of Cano son of Gartnán' and in 'The Pursuit of Diarmaid and Gráinne.' In the former tale, Créd daughter of Gúaire places a spell on her husband and the others at the feast, except for herself and Cano.[22] In the latter tale, Gráinne gives a sleeping draught to her fiancé, Fionn mac Cumhaill, and the others at the feast, and then offers herself to Oisín and Diarmaid, although they refuse her. Finally, she puts Diarmaid under bonds of 'strife and destruction' so that he must elope with her.[23]

The three types of music, *goltraí* (weeping-music), *geantraí* (laughing-music), and *suantraí* (sleeping-music), are also found in the early Irish tale, 'The Second Battle of Magh Tuireadh,' as well as in 'The Cattle-Raid of Fróech.' In the former, the Dagda's harper, Uaithne (literally 'harmony'), is carried off by the Fomorians who hang his harp on the wall. When the

Dagda arrives, he calls the harp down from the walls. It kills nine men before coming to him. The Dagda then plays the three types of music, and when the Fomorians fall asleep during the *suantraí*, the Dagda and his companions manage to escape.[24]

In 'The Cattle-Raid,' Fróech's three harpers are named Goltraiges, Gentraiges and Súantraiges. According to this account, they are three sons of Boand, the Dagda's wife. While she was in labor, Uaithne had played sad music for the first son because of her pains, happy music for the second son because of her joy at giving birth to two sons, and finally sleep-music for the third son because of the heaviness of his birth, so that she would sleep. When she awoke, she gave him the three sons as harpers, saying that they would play the three types of music, *goltraí, geantraí* and *suantraí*, for the women and cattle who would give birth under Ailill and Medb. Boand added: 'Men will die on hearing them being played.'[25]

One finds a similar sentiment being expressed in *BCF*. After Fearbhlaidh and Duibhghil come to the Burren in the form of doves, Cearbhall captures them and places them in a glass case. While he was playing his harp, 'they used to sing sad, plaintive melodies in accompaniment with his strings so that they used to put the people listening to them almost to death' (Ch. 16).

There are other verbal echoes from 'The Cattle-Raid of Fróech' in *BCF* which suggest that the author of the latter was using the former as a model. In 'The Cattle-Raid,' when Fróech and his company approach Dún Crúachan, the people smother each other in their efforts to see the company, so that sixteen men die.[26] In *BCF*, when Donnchadh Mór and his retinue of poets approach Dún Monaidh (Edinburgh), 'everyone rose up with haste to see them . . ., so that it would seem to a man who saw them that they were coming from a house on fire . . . with the amount of their haste to see the poets' (Ch. 32).

Again in 'The Cattle-Raid,' after Fróech enters Dún Crúachan with his men, he begins to play chess (fidchell) with Medb for three days and nights. To Medb it seems only a single day because of the brilliance of the precious stones among Fróech's company.[27] Earlier in the tale, their spears were described as having cusps of carbuncle and heads of precious stones which 'used to blaze at night as if they were sunbeams.'[28] In BCF, when Cearbhall appears to Fearbhlaidh in the vision, he has a 'chained, polished harp adorned with crystal and carbuncle stones in his two hands' (Ch. 5). Later, when he falls ill with a wasting sickness, Fearbhlaidh sends him a stone of healing which would light up a dark cave or a black forest at the new moon 'like a sun-ray in mid-summer' (Ch. 27).

Both J. Carney and W. Meid have discussed the topos of the stone which shines at night. According to Carney, its occurrence in 'The Cattle-Raid of Fróech' is the product of a joint borrowing from hagiographical tradition and from Isidore of Seville. In a life of St. Brigit we find St. Patrick visiting her household and preaching the word of God for three days and nights, during which time no one hungers and the sun does not set. The author of 'The Cattle-Raid' would have combined this with the passage in Isidore's Etymologiae in which carbunculus 'carbuncle' is associated with carbo 'coal.' Isidore adds that it is not conquered by night but lights up in the darkness so that it causes flames to flicker before the eyes.[29] Meid disagrees with Carney's explanation of this incident. According to him, this topos of the day which is extended, and the hunger and thirst which are kept

[26]

from a certain person, is pre-Christian, since one finds it in 'The Wooing of Étaín.' Furthermore, he suggests that the topos of the stone which lights up in the night, although it may have originally been borrowed from Isidore, was a commonplace in early Irish literature. Meid suggests that the author of 'The Cattle-Raid' may have taken it from 'the stream of common tradition of which it was a part.'[30] It is possible that the author of *BCF* may have also borrowed it from the 'common stock of storytelling,' rather than specifically from 'The Cattle-Raid,' particularly since one finds it elsewhere in the late romances.

One finds other commonplaces in *BCF*, for example, the descriptions of the main characters, which have several parallels in early Irish literature. When Séamas confronts Fearbhlaidh with the request that she tell him who is the one she loves, she changes color:

> First she was as red as valerian in early summer. Next she was as black as coal. The third time she was as white as fully-woven linen sheets (Ch. 4).

The combination red/black/white occurs frequently in both Welsh and Irish descriptions, for example, in the Welsh tale, 'Peredur the son of Efrawg,' from *The Mabinogion,* and in the Irish tale, 'The Exile of the Sons of Uisliu.'[31] Georges Dumézil has suggested an Indo-European basis for this schema: red symbolizing the warrior class (second function), black the farmer or producer class (third function), and white the priestly class (first function) of the society.[32] Although the use of coal in such a simile is fairly common, the use of valerian and linen is quite rare.

The description of Cearbhall also seems to have been modelled on early Irish examples although curiously, given the reversal of roles in the story, they are

[27]

usually descriptions of women. When Duibhghil comes to the house where Cearbhall lives:

> She found there a modest, bashful lad. he had black curly-tressed hair, and a gentle, pleasing countenance. His two cheeks were redder than embers and his lips redder than Parthian leather. His body was as white as snow, his eye as blue as a hyacinth, and the sound of his voice was as sweet as harp strings. It seemed to her that he had not completed fifteen years of age (Ch. 11).

One notices the 'repertoire-like similarity' of the first part of this description to the earlier one of him given by Fearbhlaidh to her father (Ch. 5), i.e., the curly black hair and the pleasing countenance, which is a characteristic of Irish narrative style. The author uses the same alliterative pair, *neoid náireach* ('modest, bashful') to describe the lad here as he earlier used to describe Fearbhlaidh's voice (Ch. 4). The next part of the description, the cheeks redder than embers and the lips redder than Parthian leather (*partaing* or *partlainn*, derived from *Parthica [pellis]* 'Parthian leather dyed scarlet'), is also extremely common, although the latter is more frequently found as a simile. The scribe of H[1] in fact changed the description in *BCF* to agree with this convention: 'as red as *partaing* were each of his two cheeks and his mouth.' The comparisons of Cearbhall's body to snow and his eyes to hyacinths have parallels in the description of Étaín in 'The Wooing of Étaín' and 'The Destruction of Da Derga's Hostel.' In the former her arms are said to be 'as white as the snow of a single night' and 'each of her two eyes as blue as the hyacinth.'[33] In the latter we find both these similes and the statement that 'her lips were as red as *partaing*.'[34] The comparison of Cearbhall's voice to the harp strings has a counterpart in the description of the prophetess Feidelm in 'The Cattle-Raid of Cooley' which states that 'the sweet sound of her voice and speech was as melodious as the strings of the harps plucked by the hands of masters.'[35] This description also includes the comparison of her lips to *partaing* and her skin to snow. The reference to Cearbhall's age as not more than fifteen may seem surprising at first, until one remembers that Cú Chulainn was still a beardless youth when he wooed Emer, and that he was only seventeen when he fought against the Connachtmen during the cattle-raid of Cooley.

Returning to the themes in *BCF*, we find that the two themes of *searg* (wasting sickness) and *gealtacht* (madness) are combined here as they are in 'The Sick-Bed of Cú Chulainn.' In this tale, after Cú throws his spear at the two swans, he falls asleep and sees two women who appear to him in a vision (*aisling*). They take turns beating him with horse-whips. When he awakens, he is so ill that he must remain in his sickbed (*serglige*, from *serg + lige* 'bed') for a year. Finally, he discovers that his assailants were two women from the *síodh*, Fand and her sister Lí Ban, the wife of Labraid, who offers Cú the reward of Fand for fighting against an Otherworld opponent. Cú agrees and, after slaying the opponent, sleeps with Fand. He remains with her for a month. When Fand and Cú meet later at their trysting place, Emer, Cú's wife, arrives along with fifty women. Fand relinquishes him and leaves with Manannán mac Lir, her husband. Cú sees them going away, makes three leaps into the air, and then makes three leaps until he comes to Sliabh Lúachra. 'He was a long time without drink or food, wandering through the mountains. And he used to sleep every night on Slige Midlúachra,' the road which runs through Lúachra.[36] Compare this with the description of Fearbhlaidh's madness when Cearbhall is placed in prison and sentenced to death: 'She did not recognize one person from another. She did not hear or see, she did not sleep or eat, she did not bathe or wash' (Ch. 37). Also, note Cearbhall's state when he escapes from prison and returns to Ireland: 'He became a terrible churl, so that neither friend nor companion would recognize his shape or his appearance' (Ch. 44).

In 'The Sick-Bed,' Emer comes to Conchobhar after Cú flees to Lúachra, and she tells him of Cú's state. Conchobhar sends his druids to find him, and they bring him back to Emain Macha bound hand and foot. He asks for a drink and they give him a 'drink of forgetfulness' (*deog dermait*) so that he will forget Fand. They also give Emer one so that she will forget her jealousy. Meanwhile, Manannán shakes his cloak between Fand and Cú so that they will never meet again.

In *BCF* we learn that Donnchadh Mór and the Connachtmen become concerned about Cearbhall's condition: 'They decided to bring evil sorcerers to him who would give him drinks of forgetfulness, and this was done, so that Cearbhall did not remember ever having seen Fearbhlaidh with his eyes, and he was healed from all sickness' (Ch. 45).

As mentioned above, Cearbhall suffers the sickness of despair when he marries another woman, Ailbhe, then remembers Fearbhlaidh and realizes what he has done. All his friends think that he has been enchanted by someone from the Otherworld: they ask him what delusion (*siabhradh*) or deception (*seachrán*) has overcome him (Ch. 52). He does not speak to them and they remain a fortnight hoping that 'sense would come to him.' Finally, they leave him in Aughrim of Uí Mhaine 'without sense or speech' (Ch. 53).

One of the characteristics of madness in French and British romances is that the victim is 'senseless and deprived of speech,' as in the case of Yvain.[37] Also, in these romances only one person can cure the victim of his madness, namely the woman he loves, e.g., Yseut, in the case of Tristan.[38] In *BCF* Fearbhlaidh arrives each night in the house where Cearbhall is being kept in Aughrim, along with Duibhghil, presumably to bring about his cure (Ch. 54).

Along with this theme of the madness caused from despair which can only be cured by a certain individual, the presence of the 'Tristan-style dénouement'[39] in *BCF* leads one to suspect that there has been a non-Irish influence upon the development of this romance, possibly from a French or English source. Although Alan Bruford found no apparent influences from continental romance in *BCF*,[40] I believe that the occurrence of these two themes of madness from despair and death from false report, both also associated with the Tristan romance, indicate otherwise. In addition, the non-passive roles given to the two main female characters, Fearbhlaidh and Duibhghil, show signs of a reshaping of the tradition found in early Irish literature. Séamas's willingness to allow Fearbhlaidh a choice in selecting a husband (Ch. 1) suggests a familiarity with the theoretical tenets of *amour courtois*, in which a woman allegedly has the right to choose her lover. On the other hand, women in early Irish saga often do take the initiative in love affairs, particularly in the *aitheda* or 'elopement tales,' for example, Gráinne in 'The Pursuit of Diarmaid and Gráinne' and Deirdre in 'The Exile of the Sons of Uisliu.'

In the latter tale, Deirdre, who has been raised apart in order to be married to Conchobhar, sees her foster-father skinning a calf on the snow one day, and a raven drinking its blood. She says that she desires a man who has hair the color of the raven, cheeks like the calf's blood and skin like the snow. Her foster-mother, Lebhorcham, tells her that the man who meets that description is close at hand, namely Naoise mac Uislenn. Deirdre then goes to him and convinces him to elope with her. They flee to Scotland along with his two brothers, Ainle and Ardán. However, they are deceived into returning to Ireland, where the three brothers are killed upon Conchobhar's orders. Deirdre finally kills herself while riding in a chariot, by letting herself be driven against a stone so that her head is broken.[41]

As in this tale, both lovers in *BCF* die tragically. The deaths of Cearbhall and Fearbhlaidh are symmetrical, in both cases connected with an instrument centrally involved in their love affair, namely a chessboard and a harp. Fearbhlaidh had fallen in love with Cearbhall after hearing him play his harp when he visited her in an *aisling*. Later, she became entranced while hearing him play his harp when she rested outside his window in the form of a dove. During Cearbhall's visit to her father's court, he played his harp so that everyone fell asleep and the two lovers were able to be alone. Their love affair is discovered during a chess game in which Cearbhall, sitting opposite Fearbhlaidh and her father, accidentally scratches Séamas's foot with his toe, thinking it to be Fearbhlaidh's foot (Ch. 34). He is saved from execution by the influence of his uncle, Macaomh Inse Creamha ('The Youth of Inishcraff,' a small island in Lough Corrib, Co. Galway), who persuades Séamas that Cearbhall always scratches the foot of the person with whom he is playing a game (Ch. 35). This episode, which has been described as an element of 'broad farce,' reveals a less tragic side of the romance. After Cearbhall's marriage to Ailbhe, Fearbhlaidh comes to the wedding house and carves a poem on Cearbhall's harp in her own blood, and his madness is a direct result of reading this poem. Finally, after hearing the false report of Cearbhall's death, Fearbhlaidh falls lifeless upon her chessboard, and when Cearbhall hears of Fear-bhlaidh's death, he lays his head upon his harp and dies.

In addition to the elopement theme and the tragic ending, there is another parallel between 'The Exile of the Sons of Uisliu' and *BCF*, namely the 'nurse' or 'foster mother' (*buime*). Both Lebhorcham and Duibhghil act as intermediaries in some way: Lebhorcham by informing Deirdre of the identity of her lover, and Duibhghil by searching for Fearbhlaidh's lover and then informing her when she finds him. However, the nurse or handmaid who acts as an intermediary is also found in Continental and English romance and tragedy, for example, Brangain (Brangien) in the romance of Tristan, and Juliet's nurse in *Romeo and Juliet*.

In the former, Brangain serves Tristan and Yseut the love potion thinking it wine, which causes them to fall in love. In 'Tristan's Madness' (*La Folie de Tristan*), when Tristan, posing as a fool, comes to the Cornish court, Yseut sends Brangain to him to find out who he is. Brangain intercedes for Tristan with her mistress, and finally persuades her to sleep with him, saying that she should do everything she can 'to please him' while Mark is away.[42] In *BCF* Duibhghil brings Fearbhlaidh to Finnyvara to see Cearbhall in the form of a dove. After the two women are restored to their own shapes, she realizes that Cearbhall is in love with Fearbhlaidh and so hurriedly exits, leaving the two lovers alone together (Ch. 21). This aspect of her role as 'bawd' also suggests the nurse in *Romeo and Juliet* who sends Juliet to Friar Lawrence's cell to marry Romeo, after she has already acted as a go-between in arranging the marriage (Act II, Scenes iv-v).

III THE HISTORICAL BACKGROUND

Most of the characters in *BCF* are either completely fictional or else loosely based on historical figures. Séamas is probably modelled on an early King James of Scotland, possibly James I (reigned 1401-37), although there was no Torcall (from ON. Thorkell) among the Scottish kings. Only James V had an only daughter, the future Mary Queen of Scots, who was but eight days when her father died in 1542, making it unlikely that she was the model for Fearbhlaidh.[43]

There was no Conchobhar mac Ceallaigh mhic Fhiannachta among the kings of Uí Mhaine (in present-day Cos. Galway and Roscommon), although there was a ninth-century king, Ceallach mac Fiannachta, who is given as the progenitor of the O'Kellys (Uí Cheallaigh). This Ceallach had a great-great-grandson, Conchobhar Ó Ceallaigh, who was slain in 1030, and there were several additional kings of that name, including Conchobhar Mór who died in 1268, and Conchobhar Anabaidh ('the Immature', or 'the Unripe') who died in 1403.[44]

It is generally assumed that Donnchadh Mór Ó Dálaigh represents the poet of that name who died in 1244. In the Annals of the Four Masters, Donnchadh is called 'a poet who never was and never will be surpassed.'[45] Partly because of the fame of his religious verse, some of which still survives in Irish oral tradition, he was generally supposed to have become the Abbot of Boyle (Co. Roscommon) in later life. A tree in the cemetery of Boyle was said to mark the site of his grave.[46]

In some genealogies, Donnchadh Mór was considered the ancestor of the Ó Dálaighs of Finnyvara in the Burren of Co. Clare. An anachronistic tradition maintains that Donnchadh Mór founded the bardic school there, which flourished during the fifteenth century.[47] A stone monument dedicated to Donnchadh Mór still marks the site of this school.

Concerning the identity of Donnchadh (Donogh) Mór Ó Dálaigh in *BCF*, Edward O'Reilly states in his unpublished translation of the tale:

> The author of this tale, by a poetic license, makes Donogh Mór an actor in his story, and the father also of his hero, Carroll, which bids defiance to all historical truth, for Donogh Mór Ó Dálaigh was Abbot of Boyle and had no children. But there is reason to suppose that this tale was written subsequent to the year 1404, for in that year died a Carroll O'Daly who was much celebrated as the Poet of . . . Corcomroe; and many of his poems and tales are still remembered. Now as the author of this tale has made Donogh Mór the father of the hero, so he has transformed Boyle to Burren, in Northern Corcomroe, where the Carroll O'Daly, last mentioned, flourished . . . It is therefore likely that Carroll was the poet the author intended for the hero of his tale; and therefore it would not have been written earlier than the middle of the fifteenth century.[48]

The Annal entry for 1404 states: 'Cearbhall Ó Dálaigh, *ollamh* of Corcomroe, and Domhnall, the son of Donnchadh Ó Dálaigh, who was called *Bolg an Dána* ('the Receptacle of Poetry') died.'[49] Dáithí Ó hÓgáin has suggested that the author of *BCF* may have been familiar with this entry and that may have misinterpreted the patronymic as referring to both

[35]

poets, whereas it only refers to Domhnall.[50] However, I doubt that the author of BCF, who was possibly an Ó Dálaigh poet himself, would have confused this Donnchadh with Donnchadh Mór, who had died 160 years before this date.

Roderick O'Flaherty, in *Ogygia* (1684), refers to Macaomh Inse Creamha ('the Youth of Inishcraff') as 'a memorable antient magician,'[51] who got his name from the island of Inishcraff in Lough Corrib, although O'Flaherty does not mention that the 'Youth' was an Ó Dálaigh. Joseph Walker, in *Historical Memoirs of the Irish Bards* (1786), mistakenly identified Macaomh Inse Creamha with Cearbhall, basing this on his misinterpretation of the section of BCF in which the 'Youth' appears (Ch.35). In the section entitled, 'Memoirs of Cormac Common,' Walker presents the misinformation that 'Carroll O'Daly (commonly called *Mac-Caomh Insi Cneamha*)' was 'brother to Donough More O'Daly, a man of such consequence in Connaught about two centuries ago' [ca. 1586].[52] He proceeds to give Cormac Common's version of the folktale of the seventeenth-century Cearbhall Ó Dálaigh and Eleanor Kavanagh, which includes the composition of the song, 'Eibhlín, a rúin.'

Walker's misidentification of the Cearbhall in BCF not only with Macaomh Inse Creamha, the brother of Donnchadh Mór, but also with the later Cearbhall of Irish folk tradition, was accepted by James Hardiman in *Irish Minstrelsy* (1831), an acceptance which helped to perpetuate the error. Later writers, including T. F. O'Rahilly,[53] wrongly assumed that Cormac Common, a poet in his own right, had provided this information, whereas in fact Walker had provided the 'biographical information' about Cearbhall based on his knowledge of BCF, adding this to Common's rendition of the folktale and song, thereby initiating the mistaken belief that the two Cearbhalls were a single poet.

In addition to Donnchadh Mór's fame as a poet, and the tradition that he was the ancestor of the Ó Dálaigh poets of Corcomroe, there may be another reason why the author of BCF associated Cearbhall with the Donnchadh Mór Ó Dálaigh who died at Boyle in 1244. The Ó Dálaighs of Corcomroe were the hereditary poets first of the O'Loughlin (Ó Lochlainn) family of the Burren, and later of the O'Briens of Co. Clare. One of the O'Loughlins, Conghalach Ó Lochlainn, was the bishop of Corcomroe from 1281 to 1300.[54] Some time before this, Conchobhar Mór Ó Ceallaigh (O'Kelly), king of Uí Mhaine from 1247 to 1268, had married as his second wife, Derbhail, daughter of Ó Lochlainn of the Burren, who bore him Donnchadh Muimhneach ('the Munsterman') Ó Ceallaigh, 'obviously so called from having been fostered in Munster, probably by his maternal grandfather,' Ó Lochlainn of the Burren.[55] This Donnchadh was the ancestor of the subsequent O'Kelly kings of Uí Mhaine. Among his descendants was Tadhg Ruadh Ó Ceallaigh of Callow, son of Maelseachlainn Ó Ceallaigh (d. 1464), the brother of Aedh na Coille Ó Ceallaigh of Aughrim (d. 1469). This Tadhg Ruadh married Raghnailt Ní Bhriain (O'Brien), who brought the first Ó Dálaigh poet to Uí Mhaine from Corcomroe (ca. 1450?). This poet, the ancestor of Lord Dunsandle, traced his descent from Donnchadh Mór Ó Dálaigh,[56] and was no doubt familiar with the traditions surrounding Cearbhall, ollamh of Corcomroe, who had died only some fifty years before.

If Raghnailt's poet composed BCF, possibly for his patroness after her marriage, it would not be surprising that he would make the hero of the romance, Cearbhall, the son of his own ancestor, Donnchadh Mór Ó

[37]

Dálaigh. In addition, since Donnchadh Mór had been a near contemporary of Tadhg Ruadh's ancestor, Conchobhar Mór Ó Ceallaigh, the poet might have deliberately set the romance in the thirteenth century and used the name Conchobhar for the king of Uí Mhaine in order to flatter his patroness's husband. On the other hand, the presence of a Conchobhar Anabaidh Ó Ceallaigh who died in 1403, the year before the death of Cearbhall, *ollamh* of Corcomroe, suggests that the author of BCF might have been dealing with an historical tradition associating Cearbhall with Uí Mhaine.

Further evidence that BCF was composed by someone familiar with Connacht, and particularly with the Uí Mhaine territory in Cos. Galway and Roscommon, is provided from the fact that, with the exception of Finnyvara and Corcomroe in the Burren (Co. Clare) and Dún Monaidh (Edinburgh) in Scotland, all the place-names mentioned in the romance are located in the province of Connacht.

The Burren itself is only a few miles from the Galway border, and doubtless there were strong connections between NW. Clare and Galway, as can be seen from the marriages of the O'Loughlins (and O'Briens) with the O'Kellys. The Burren remained an important cultural center throughout the Middle Ages because, in addition to the Ó Dálaigh bardic school and Corcomroe Abbey, there was a cathedral at Kilfenora and a Brehon law school at Cahermacnaghten under the O'Davoren (Ó Dubhdábhoireann) family.

Dún Monaidh is usually described as *baile ríogh Alban* ('the king of Scotland's place') in BCF. Originally, it seems to have been used loosely to denote the seat of the Gaelic king of Scotland wherever he might be at a certain time.[57] By the fifteenth century, it was usually associated with Edinburgh, and in 1565 we find John Carswell writing that Dún Monaidh was another name for Edinburgh (*dún Edin darab comhainm dún Monaidh*).[58]

Regarding the place-names in Connacht mentioned in *BCF*, Donnchadh Mór's brother, Macaomh Inse Creamha, is associated with Inishcraff in Lough Corrib (Co. Galway). Donnchadh Mór himself conspires with the Connachtmen to end Cearbhall's love sickness (Ch. 45). Afterwards, the nobles of Connacht attend Cearbhall's wedding with Ó Ceallaigh's daughter in Uí Mhaine. When Cearbhall goes mad, he is brought to Aughrim, also in Co. Galway. Fearbhlaidh and Duibhghil visit him there and on the shore of the River Suck (on the border of Cos. Galway and Roscommon). Finally, two Connachtmen from Cruachan (Rathcroghan, Co. Roscommon) tell Fearbhlaidh that Cearbhall is dead, and after Cearbhall's death the Connachtmen in all four corners of the province grieve for him, taking neither food nor drink for three days and nights. This reminds one of the conclusion of 'The Death of Aife's One Son', when, after Connla's death at the hands of his father, Cú Chulainn, 'for the space of three days and nights no calf in Ulster was let go to its cow on account of his death.'[59] The description of Fearbhlaidh's funeral rites also finds a parallel in this story.

Here follows a map showing the places in Ireland associated with *BCF*, along with adjacent sites mentioned in this introduction:

[39]

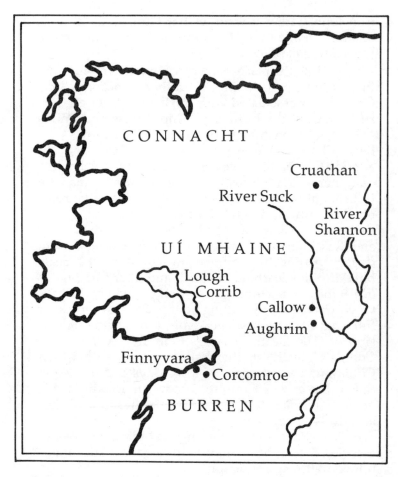

Figure 2. A Map of Irish Places Associated with *Bás Chearbhaill 7 Fhearbhlaidhe*.

The poetry in *BCF* suggests that the romance was written by a *file*, or professional poet, such as the Ó Dálaigh poet of Raghnailt Ní Bhriain. Four of the six poems are in *deibhí* meter, one is in *ae fhreislí*, and the remaining poem is in a mixture of *deibhí* and *rannaíocht*. Of the four poems in *deibhi*, the two which are recited by Cearbhall are in good *dán díreach*, or 'strict meter' (Chs. 13, 48). The author of *BCF* may have consciously distinguished between the poems recited by Cearbhall, who is described as a *file* (Ch. 15), and those recited by Fearbhlaidh who, as a woman, would be an amateur poet at best, and therefore more likely to compose in *ógláchas* than in *dán díreach*. Of the remaining two poems in *BCF*, both recited by Cearbhall, the poem in *ae fhreislí* (Ch. 55) is in *ógláchas*, whereas the mixed *deibhí-rannaíocht* poem (Ch. 50) is metrically corrupt.

The author of *BCF* devotes a great deal of attention to the emotions of Cearbhall and Fearbhlaidh, which are often expressed through their poetry. The author's interest in the vicissitudes of his heroine's emotional states — her anguish in seeking to find the man she loves, her joy when she discovers who he is, her madness when he is imprisoned, her grief when he marries another, and finally her despair when she hears that he is dead — supports the view that he may have intended this romance for a female audience. If *BCF* was written by the Ó Dálaigh poet for his patroness, Raghnailt Ní Bhriain, one should not wonder at the fact that he concerned himself so much with themes pertaining to love. An analogous situation exists in the romances written by Chrétien de Troyes for Marie, Countess of Champagne, between 1160 and 1172, which deal predominately with the subject of love, often from the woman's perspective. In the prologue to *Lancelot,* or *Le Chevalier de la Charrete,* in fact, Chrétien states that he is only trying to carry out Marie's 'concern and intention.'[60]

Generally the quality of the poetry in the late medieval Irish romances is not particularly high. Therefore, it is unusual to find that the poetry in *BCF* is as good as it is. In *Gaelic Folktales and Medieval Romances,* Alan Bruford suggests that the rewards for writing romances were not as high as those for writing bardic eulogies.[61] However, if *BCF* was composed for a noblewoman, the author may have expected to be generously rewarded. Perhaps Donnchadh's reward for the *dán* (bardic poem) he composed for Séamas in *BCF,* 'one hundred of each sort of cattle, . . . one hundred ounces of each metal, and the king's own dress, cup and ivory-hilted sword' (Ch. 33), although undoubtedly exaggerated, reflects the author's idea of a suitable reward for his own composition!

If the author of *BCF* did compose the romance for an Ó Ceallaigh, he might well have expected a fine reward. The family were well known for their generosity to poets. For example, in 1351, according to the Annals of Clonmacnoise, Uilliam, son of Donnchadh Muimhneach Ó Ceallaigh, invited all the 'Irish poets, brehons, bards, harpers, gamesters,' etc., to his house at Christmas, where he entertained them and rewarded them as they left, so that they extolled him for his bounty. One of them composed a poem beginning, 'The poets of Ireland to one house,' before leaving.[62]

According to this poem, Uilliam Ó Ceallaigh held this feast in Galey (Gaille) castle on the shore of Lough Ree (Co. Roscommon). In addition to building this castle, he founded the abbey of Kilconnell in 1353 and also built the near-by castle of Callow (Caladh), shown on the above map. It was to Callow castle that

Tadhg Ruadh Ó Ceallaigh brought his wife, Raghnailt Ní Bhriain, around the year 1450, and perhaps it was here that *BCF* was composed about the same time. If so, the Ó Dálaigh poet/author may have had Tadhg Ruadh's wedding feast in mind as the model for Ailbhe's wedding in *BCF*.

At any rate, Callow is only a few miles from Aughrim and the River Suck, so that the author of *BCF* would have been familiar with both if he lived at Callow. In addition, Tadhg Ruadh's uncle was lord of Aughrim, as mentioned above. If the romance was composed in Co. Galway in the mid-fifteenth century, it is not difficult to imagine that copies of it were brought to Ulster and Munster during the next two hundred years. It would be from these copies that the seventeenth-century manuscripts derive.

Regarding the poetry in *BCF*, the two poems in *deibhí* recited by Cearbhall (Chs. 28, 57), by far the longest in the romance, being seven and fourteen quatrains respectively, may represent works actually ascribed to the historical poet who died in 1404. Both of these poems are quite well executed, and manage to sustain a single image or conceit throughout.

In the former, which begins, 'I found a stone to be a poisonous stone,' the poet uses the fiction that the healing stone which he has received from Fearbhlaidh, although it has cured him, has also 'maddened' him. The stone becomes a metaphor for the woman who sent it, continually reminding him of her. He thinks of her neck when he recalls that the stone's silken cord had been around it. He remembers her breasts when he realizes that the stone had been between them, and he 'sees' the reflection of her breast in it. He adds that no one, except the person who gave it, will ever receive the stone from him.

The second poem which begins, 'Alas your hand,

Duibhghil,' deals entirely with Duibhghil's hand which, according to the romance, has been broken by the cowherd of Aughrim. Cearbhall says that everyone is grieving for her hand, including 'the royal sons of the kings of Ireland,' warriors and women. He refers to the hand as 'a pillow of high kings,' and describes it filling a satin sleeve embroidered with gold and silver. He relates how it dispensed jewels and captured 'gilded chessmen.' Finally, he mentions his own grief, saying that he no longer enjoys music, poetic skill or discourse, and that the injury to her hand has also wounded him 'mortally.'

This poem may have originally been composed by the historical poet as a love poem, and then incorporated into the romance by the author or a later redactor. Although the poem is not found in the three early Ulster manuscripts (A^1, H^1 and P^1), it is found in the earliest Munster text (M^1), written by Eóghan Ó Caoimh in 1684, as well as in the subsequent Munster manuscripts. This may be the result either of the poem's interpolation into the text by Ó Caoimh, or else of the poem's deliberate exclusion by the Ulster scribes, perhaps because of the considerable length of the poem, and the fact that it causes a break in the narrative flow of the romance.

M^1 contains two quatrains (7 and 11) not found in the later Munster texts (e.g., K^1, P^2 and E^1, which Eoghan Ó Neachtain used for his edition of the poem in 'Tochmarc Fhearbhlaide'[63]).For this reason, I have used M^1 as the basis for my translation of this poem, with emendations based on Ó Neachtain's edition. The later Munster copies seem to derive from K^1, written in 1700, since they use Mac Donnchadha's title for the romance and also include a version of 'Alas your hand' very similar to his. The four nineteenth-century copies (M^2, E^2, D^1 and A^2) stem directly from E^1, the copy made by Mícheál Óg Ó Longáin.

The Munster scribes were probably familiar with a different recension of the romance from the one which forms the basis for the Ulster version of the tale. Only one Ulster manuscript (B¹) contains the poem, 'Alas your hand.' In addition, this is the only Ulster text to use the 'Munster' title for the romance, 'Tochmharc Fhearbhlaidhe,' which suggests that the scribe, Seaghán Gaillidhe, made his copy from a Munster manuscript.

The remaining poems in *BCF* are short, lyrical compositions, which the author of the romance intended as occasional pieces. The first quatrain of the *deibhí* poem recited by Fearbhlaidh which begins, 'Duibhghil, do you hear the uproar,' is found as an example of *óglachas* in a seventeenth-century Irish grammar, *Graiméar Uí Mhaolchonaire*, which was quite likely written in the Franciscan College at Louvain. A¹ was part of the collection at Louvain at least as early as 1630,[64] which suggests that the author of the grammar may have been familiar with the romance from that source, although the quatrain does not correspond exactly to the version found in A¹.[65]

V THE LATER TRADITION OF THE ROMANCE

Several poems written between 1650 and 1700 deal specifically with the story of Cearbhall and Fearbhlaidh, or else allude to it, indicating the continued popularity of *BCF*, particularly among Ulster poets. In a lament written upon the exile of the Cavan leader, Pilib son of Aodh, son of Sir John O'Reilly, who left for Spain in 1653, the poet compares Pilib's leaving Ireland to Cearbhall's leaving Fearbhlaidh.[66] In an elegy on a dog named Farbhlaidh which belonged to 'Mairghréag daughter of Conn,' the poet refers to 'the first

Farbhlaidh who brought disfavor on poets,' presumably because love for her led Cearbhall to his death.[67] In addition, we find poems by the Louth poet, Séamas Dall Mac Cuarta,[68] the Armagh poet, Pádraig Mac a Liondain,[69] and the Cavan poet, Cormac McPharlane,[70] all dating to ca. 1700, which deal with the figures of Cearbhall and Fearbhlaidh.

Also dating from the early 1700's, we find two manuscripts of a late redaction of the romance entitled, *Eachtra Abhlaighe inghine ríogh Alban agus Chearbhaill mhic Dhonnchadha Mhóir Uí Dhála ó Fhinebheara* ('The Adventure of Abhlach daughter of the king of Scotland and of Cearbhall son of Donnchadh Mór Ó Dálaigh from Finnyvara'), in which the heroine's name has been changed from Fearbhlaidh to Abhlach.[71] This redaction was probably composed in Ulster during the late seventeenth or early eighteenth century.

In addition, there exist two unpublished English translations of the romance, both dating from the late eighteenth century. One of them, entitled, 'The Adventures of Faravla, Princess of Scotland, and Carval O'Daly, son of Donogh Mor,'[72] is attributed to Joseph Walker, although this is questionable since it does not agree with the excerpts from the tale included in his *Historical Memoirs of the Irish Bards*. For example, in the manuscript Donnchadh's brother, although he is not named, frees Donnchadh and Cearbhall, whereas in *Historical Memoirs* Donnchadh's brother is identified with Cearbhall, as mentioned above. At anjy rate, this translation is a conflation of the two versions of the romance, both *BCF* and *Eachtra Abhlaighe*. Sir Walter Scott was apparently familiar with this translation since he cites it in his notes for 'The Gay Goss Hawk' in *Minstrelsy of the Scottish Border* (1802).[73] The other translation of *BCF*, entitled, 'The

Tale of Farbhlaidh, daughter of James son of Turcaill, king of Scotland, and Carroll O'Daly,'[74] was made by Edward O'Reilly ca. 1800, and was probably based on a version of the romance such as that found in P[1].

As well as the two editions of the romance mentioned earlier, the tale has appeared in print on two other occasions. The version found in B[2] was edited in *The Irish Rosary* 17) (1913) as 'Pósadh Chearbhaill Uí Dhálaigh,' although the poem, 'Alas your hand,' not found in that text, was provided from Ó Neachtain's edition in *Ériu*. Ó Neachtain himself published a translation of the romance into Modern Irish as *Tochmharc Fhearbhlaidhe* in Dublin in 1916.

NOTE ON THE TRANSLATION

This is the first English translation of the romance to appear in print. In undertaking this translation I have tried to use the best readings from the three early Ulster manuscripts, based on the edition of A^1 and H^1 by Walsh, and of P^1 by Ó Neachtain. Although I have relied primarily on A^1, I have used H^1 and P^1 when they seemed to preserve readings closer to the original form of the romance. In the case of the poem, 'Alas your hand,' I have based my translation on M^1 with variant readings from the manuscripts used in Ó Neachtain's edition, as mentioned earlier. In translating the romance I have attempted to remain as close as possible to the original without sacrificing sense, so that the end product is, I hope, fairly literal without being slavish.

THE DEATH OF CEARBHALL AND FEARBHLAIDH

1] ONCE SÉAMAS MAC TURCAILL WAS KING OF SCOTLAND. This Séamas was a noble fellow both in form and wisdom and family, since he was descended from the race of Cairbre Rioghfhada son of Conaire. Séamas had an only daughter: Fearbhlaidh was her name. She completely surpassed the women of the world of her time in appearance, nobility and good breeding. Among the girl's accomplishments, she was strongly- and truly-learned in several different languages. Also among her talents, she used to sing plaintive strains of music. The form of any woman seemed like pure black charcoal from burnt horn which has been submerged in water compared with her form. Western Europe was full of affection and lasting love for her. Countless were the number whom she refused to marry. Love for her filled everyone so greatly that both an illustrious high-king and the chief of a tribe alike used to ask for her. That whole affair was pointless for them. Séamas had such love for the maiden that he did not cause her to marry involuntarily. The maiden moreover did not set her eye on any man at all. Everyone was filled then with hatred for the king. It seemed to them that the king himself prevented them from wooing the girl.

2] The honorable high-king worried greatly at the number of enemies and the amount of foes the girl had made for him. The king called Fear-bhlaidh aside to him one day in a secret room. 'Well indeed, dear daughter,' he said, 'I have no child or posterity but you; in spite of this, I would prefer that you had not been born from your mother's womb, for you have greatly worn out my strength and ruined my sovereignty; since everyone has attacked my territory across its borders in revenge and in retribution against me for the shame and the insult you have brought on the noble families of good stock who are in Western Europe. That is not what we thought likely while raising you as a child, but rather to get many friends and allies from you, daughter. However,' said the high-king, 'no longer disturb us now, for I swear by the elements visible and invisible that whatever man at all you desire, I will give him to you without hindrance. I give my word that I would sooner give you to the son of a slave or to any of the lowest blood in Scotland rather than continue in the state which I am in regarding your courtship. Speak now, daughter,' he said, 'and tell me the truth.'

3] 'Father,' she said, 'what do you want me to say?'

'I want,' said the father, 'you to tell me, without lie or deceit, who is the man most pleasing to you on the earth.'

4] Many colours came to her after this. First she was as red as valerian in early summer. Next she was as black as coal. The third time she was as white as fully-woven linen sheets. Death swoons almost came upon her. The maiden spoke afterwards with a modest and bashful voice.

5] 'Dear father,' she said, 'I give you my word that I do not know who is the man in the world to whom I have given my love, but I have already loved a man, though I do not know who he is.'

'How is that, daughter?' said the high-king.

'Once I was alone on my sun-roof,' said the girl,'when a mantle of sleep fell upon me. While I was there, there was revealed to me a young, beardless youth near me beside the flockbed. He had a purple, quadrangular cloak around him, black curly-tressed hair, a gentle, pleasing countenance, a chained, polished harp adorned with crystal and carbuncle stones in his two hands, and he was playing the harp while his pure vocal cords were set in accompaniment to the musical strains, so that he stole my life from me. Dear father,' she said, 'I was not able to join my mind or my heart to another man after him, and I shall not be able until I see him again.'

6] 'Fearbhlaidh,' said the high-king, 'ignore him and do not heed that Otherworld phantom or that nocturnal destruction.'

'Father,' she said, 'that is something which is not within my strength or my powers, and it is not right for you to reproach and accuse me about him.'

'Oh alas,' said the father, 'I am sorry for that inheritance of woe which your ancestress left you, namely Étaín daughter of Eochraidh, the wife of Eochaid Airem, and the other Étaín who was her daughter, and moreover Mes Buachalla, daughter of Eochaid, the mother of Conaire son of Eterscél, whom you are following. I am sorry moreover that the nature of Baillgheal daughter of Mugh Lámha is coming through you, namely your deceitful malicious kinswoman from whom came Ireland's ruin.'

7] Fearbhlaidh however made little sense of these words. The king became silent, and began to grieve and complain. 'Stop, father,' she said, 'I shall find out about that man for you before the year comes to its end, and I shall do your will if he be not found.' They bade farewell to one another after that.

8] The maiden went to her room and called her nurse to her, namely Duibhghil daughter of Dubhdhoire, a woman learned in magical arts, for Duibhghil was able to adopt every shape from that of the sea whale to the midge. Fearbhlaidh told her about the giving of her love, and her father's advice to her, the description of the one to whom she had given her love, both in form, class and dress, and what she had promised to do if she did not find out about that man by the end of a year.

9] 'Long you awaited to tell me that,' said Duibhghil, 'but be of good cheer, Fearbhlaidh,' she said. 'If that man be in the three parts of the world (Europe, Asia or Africa), I shall bring news of him to you by the end of that period of time.'

10] Duibhghil bade farewell to her charge after that, and she went to her dwelling where she kept her magical instruments. She put a blast of magical wind under herself so that she would encompass Ireland or Scotland, both the seas and the lands, in the space of a single day. Equally well Duibhghil searched the meetings and the assemblies and the secret hidden houses which were for keeping wealth and treasures. She went like that, throughout Ireland and Scotland, until she reached Finnyvara in the Burren. That was the Finnyvara which was the only center of learning of the poets of Ireland and Scotland at that time, for there were one hundred fifty students learning poetry and literary skills in every one of the four branches of poetic knowledge from Donnchadh Mór Ó Dálaigh in the place we mentioned.

11] While she was there, she heard the sound of a harp behind her in the cubicle of one of the houses to which she had gone. She went up to find out who was there. She found there a modest, bashful lad. He had black curly-tressed hair and a gentle, pleasing countenance. His two cheeks were redder than embers and his lips redder than Parthian leather. His body was as white as snow, his eyes as blue as a hyacinth, and the sound of his voice was as sweet as harp strings. It seemed to her that he had not completed fifteen years of age. However, he did not notice her, because she had not gone there in her own shape. She remained a long while watching him and listening to him as if she were a student of the school, and everyone likewise coming to him and away from him, like a swarm of bees gathering their household store in the truly-beautiful days of autumn, and himself alternately entertaining and instructing them.

12] Truly indeed,' said Duibhghil, 'you are my quest, young lad of many skills,' and she heard everyone immediately giving his surname and his first name, so that she had complete tidings of him. She went off then until she reached Edinburgh in Scotland.

13] At that time Fearbhlaidh was on the battlements of her sun-roof, and she recognised Duibhghil. The signs of death almost came upon her with her joy and gladness, and she recited this poem:

> Duibhghil has good news
> a short while she was away.
> She would never come to me
> until she obtained news of my love.

Fortunate is her charge,
my blessing on my nurse.
Duibhghil daughter of Dubhdhoire
found news of my love for me.

By my soul, I was not worthy
to be nursed by her.
No king or prince managed
to seek breasts as good as hers.

14] Her nurse greeted the girl after that. Fearbhlaidh answered her very joyfully. There was a
long silence when fear did not allow Fearbhlaidh
to ask news.

15] 'How far did you go from that day to this?'
asked Fearbhlaidh. 'You were out for a short
while, since it is a month from today since you left
home,' she said.

'A short while indeed,' said Duibhghil, 'and I
searched southern and northern Scotland, both
the sea and the land, the islands and the islets,
and I also searched the four great provinces of Ireland (Ulster, Leinster, Munster and Connacht)
and most of the other province (Meath).'

'Did you find the one I seek?' asked Fearbhlaidh.

'If I did,' said Duibhghil, 'it would be better for
you that I had not, for the one I found there is not
a spouse suitable for your race, namely a skilful,
clever-worded poet and a fine man greatly
rewarded for poetry, in the west of Ireland.'

'What is his family or kin?' asked Fearbhlaidh.

'He is a son of Donnchadh Mór Ó Dálaigh,' said Duibhghil.

'By my soul indeed, it would not have been possible for him to have a better father,' said Fearbhlaidh, 'since the high-king of Ireland or of Scotland was not his father. Dear Duibhghil,' said Fearbhlaidh, 'would it be the illustrious Cearbhall, whom we have heard is his son, who was there?'

'It is certainly he,' said Duibhghil.

'Gentle nurse, since everything is in your power, take me tonight without fail to see that man who has troubled me deeply.'

'Give me your word to come back with me again.'

'I do,' said Fearbhlaidh.

16] Duibhghil struck them both with a wand of magical transformation and made them into two bright shining doves. They went off to the Burren in northern Corcomroe. They landed after that on the glass in front of Cearbhall in his sleeping-chamber. Cearbhall was then entertaining his companions between the two sleeping periods. Fearbhlaidh recognizsed him at the first tinkling of his music. Fearbhlaidh and Duibhghil fell asleep on the window ledge because of the music. They perceived nothing the next morning until Cearbhall seized each of them in his two hands. Cearbhall called boastingly to the students who were inside and showed them the windfall, and he made a glass case for them finally. They used to consume the food and drink which was served to them. While Cearbhall was playing his harp they used to sing sad, plaintive melodies in accompaniment with the strings so that they used to put the people listening to them almost to death. They were like that for six weeks until the news of the doves reached commonly to the neighbouring territories.

17] But one time Cearbhall and they were alone in the room, and one of the doves spoke to him in a human voice. 'Well indeed, Cearbhall,' she said, 'do you know who we are and what has brought us to you?'

'I do not,' said Cearbhall.

'You will find out,' said the bird, 'if you give your word to us not to harm us and also to release us from here, and you will have a good regard for it.'

18] Cearbhall gave his word to that. Duibhghil told him all their circumstances, including the seeing of the vision, the refusal of the many courtships, the king's reproach to his daughter, Duibhghil's journey to see himself, and their coming together in the shapes of doves on that visit.

19] 'What reward shall I get for releasing you from me?' asked Cearbhall.

'Whatever you wish without injury to ourselves,' they said.

'Go into your own shapes before me then,' he

said.

20]   They did that moreover. As soon as he saw Fearbhlaidh, he fixed the point of his eye on her form, and various colors came upon him. A small drool came from his tongue, and neither of them spoke to the other.

21]   'Is this great silence on you because of me?' asked Duibhghil. As she was saying this she leapt out of the fortress window in the form of a dove.

22]   Cearbhall pulled Fearbhlaidh towards him over the side of the flockbed, and he put his hands around her neck and kissed her passionately. They were like that for three days and three nights without food or drink, without sleeping or resting, and without sin or blame. The third day, however, Duibhghil came to speak with them.

23]   'Well,' she said, 'it does not seem to you that you have been here long, although it has been long, Fearbhlaidh,' said Duibhghil. 'Remember your promise to me, and let us make for your home.'

'Let us do so,' said Fearbhlaidh. They went until they came to the place of the king of Scotland.

24]   It had been heard in all of Europe that Fearbhlaidh and her nurse were in the fairy mounds, so that people fainted from joy at finding them. Cearbhall, however was filled with diseases and many illnesses so that he could not be cured.

25. That news was heard in Ireland and in Scotland, and it was reported before the king and Fearbhlaidh; and the girl had a noble, honorable stone from which came the cure of every evil and every illness, and she said:

26] 'Dear father,' said the girl, 'if you give permission to me, I would send that noble stone which heals diseased and sick people to the son of the chief-poet of Ireland and Scotland.'

'I give it,' said the king, 'and my blessing with it.'

27] The stone reached Cearbhall and a princely treasure was found in it for, if it were in a dark cave or in the blackness of a forest at the new moon, the light which came from it would be like a sun-ray in mid-summer. Cearbhall arose upon receiving the stone, and he was without sickness or disease, and he recited this poem:

28] I found a stone to be a poisonous stone;
it troubled the bloom of my appearance.
My mind was able to affirm
that I was maddened by that gem.

A woman gave me from her royal hand
a stone and a bright cross.
Wretched the seal, the stone and the cross;
oh alas, that I was not refused.

The silk frontlet under the stone she put
around my neck with her slender hand.
The neck from which she took the string
enraged my mind with its beauty.

Och, sharply the stone of the woman who ruined
my mind
went through my skin.
The holy stone of the pearls used to be
in the company of her two pointed breasts.

However often the beautiful, blue-spotted pearl
is sought from me,
those who seek it do not get it
over the one who gave the pearl.

Excellent is the shape of the beautiful,
gold-branched stone
in the midst of the assembly,
the purple stone and the white neck,
the reflection of her breast in its center.

Each time I see the stone
I remember the stately woman.
Worthy is the one to whom the stone is company;
another stone like it I have not found.

29] After that, Cearbhall wrote down the poem.
Her sent it with Fearbhlaidh's messenger, and
the amount of joy which the girl had from the
little gift of poetry and literary skill cannot be
told.
30] Cearbhall, however, began to petition the
fine poet, namely Donnchadh Mór, to go on a
poetic circuit to Scotland. Donnchadh Mór was
loathe to do that; however, he agreed with him to

go there. He was three years planning that journey, and the king used to expect each season that Donnchadh would go to him.

31]   As for Cearbhall and Fearbhlaidh, they did not spend six weeks of that time without jewels and messengers being sent back and forth between them. Ireland and Scotland were full of reports of these two: Cearbhall for nobility and for courtliness, Fearbhlaidh moreover for generosity and for beauty.

32]   As for Donnchadh Mór, his son insisted on going on the poetic circuit to Scotland, and he brought with him a chosen band of poets in his company. In addition, Cearbhall brought with him twelve of the best students who were in Ireland, and a harp and chessboard with each of them. They were all equal in age and in appearance. Their adventures are not reported until they reached the court of the high-king of Scotland. A man of the household told the king that the band of poets was on the lawn of the fortress. He told the king the condition they were in. the king was drinking ale at that time. Everyone rose up at once with haste to see them. They threw the goblets and the cups from their hands around the vats of ale. Others of them broke the glass goblets lest they should not reach the doors, so that it would seem to a man who saw them that they were coming from a house on fire, or that the columns and pillars of the castle were falling on them with the amount of their haste to see the poets.

The king welcomed Donnchadh with his retinue, and he did not speak to Cearbhall, but brought him along through sheer folly and placed him under his own protection in his royal seat. Fearbhlaidh and Duibhghil were on either side of him, and Donnchadh himself beside the king, and the poets out from there in their appropriate places according to age. After that had been arranged for them, the king asked Cearbhall to take his harp so that it would be a joy of mind and spirit for everyone to hear it. Cearbhall took up his harp and played reels and jigs and melodies, namely weeping-music, laughing-music and sleeping-music, so that the poets and princes and likewise the hosts were in a dead and long-lasting sleep, except for Cearbhall, Fearbhlaidh and Duibhghil. The three began to complain of their anxiety and their unbearable suffering to one another. Fearbhlaidh began to revile and bitterly reproach destiny and the time of her conception and birth, and her damnable disposition towards Cearbhall, until Cearbhall began to soothe her with gentle, affable words and pleasant, cheerful speech, and Duibhghil began to do likewise.

33] They were like that until the middle of the next day. Each one awoke at the same time and put his hand on the same cup of ale. They were like that until the end of seven nights and days drinking and in great mirth, without making beds, without song, without music, but only drinking ale and consuming food. A poem by

[62]

Donnchadh Mór was accepted on the seventh day, and one hundred of each sort of cattle were given to him, one hundred ounces of each metal, and the king's own dress, cup and ivory-hilted sword.

34] The king asked Cearbhall for harp music. Cearbhall took the harp and he played weeping-music, laughing-music and finally pure sleeping-music, so that they were all sleeping from that time until the same time on the next day, except for Cearbhall and Fearbhlaidh. The king awoke then and asked Cearbhall for a chess game. Both of them played and Cearbhall won seven games without missing a single move. Cearbhall's foot was extended below the chessboard. Fearbhlaidh was beside the king, and the king's foot was extended below the other side of the chessboard. Cearbhall thought that Fearbhlaidh's foot was there and he began to scratch the king's foot with his nails. The king felt that, and he was filled with anger and astonishment upon learning Cearbhall's intention towards the girl, so that he arose from the chess game. He called the nobles of his household to him, and he told them the circumstances of the poet and the girl. They resolved to kill Donnchadh with his retinue and his son.

35] However, Donnchad Mór had a shrewd man for a brother, namely 'The Youth of Inishcraff,' and he found out each secret, hidden dealing which there was between people, and he saw that his brother and nephew were in that strait, and he went to help them. The length of time he was on the road is not reported until he reached the place of the king of Scotland, and he found the king with his household in that council. He greeted them and he asked the king for news of Donnchadh and Cearbhall, and the king said that they were there. The Youth asked the king if Cearbhall had been playing with him, and the king said that he had been. 'Woe to him who was in that game,' said the Youth, 'for it would be easier for someone to be in battle or in combat than to be playing with him, for he has never played a game without scratching the one who was nearest with his toe-nails.'

36] The Youth went from them after saying these words. 'Almighty God, great is the treachery we thought to do to the poets,' said the king.

'Truly indeed,' said the household.

37] They went off then. Donnchadh took his leave from the king. The king permitted him although he was reluctant to do so, but he kept Cearbhall and his company. Cearbhall moreover was a whole year on that visit. The final month of the year, the affair between Cearbhall and Fearbhlaidh was revealed, so that they could not deny it. Cearbhall was arrested and put into a stone prison. Bonds and fetters were placed on him, and they decided to put him to death. Fearbhlaidh was indeed wretched because of that. She did not recognize one person from another.

She did not hear or see, she did not sleep or eat, she did not bathe or wash. She spent six weeks in that plight until she finally realized how she would go to help her friend.

38] She went one day to the prison. The girl asked the guard if he would let her in, and he refused her twice. She made him a large gift of gold and silver, and he finally agreed to let her in. Fearbhlaidh went in and sat on Cearbhall's right side and kissed him. then Fearbhlaidh looked at the door-keeper.

39 'Well indeed, friend,' she said, 'go from us to the prison door and do not remain watching us now, for we have no way of escape but that one door.'

40] The door-keeper went from them after these words were spoken. Fearbhlaidh quickly took off her own clothes and put them on Cearbhall, and she put his mantle around herself, and she said to him: 'Go out in my appearance,' she said, 'and leave between me and the king whatever revenge he will take on me.'

41] He went out and bade farewell to the door-keeper, and he commanded him earnestly to treat well the captive who was in the prison, namely Cearbhall. The door-keeper promised that he would. Cearbhall went hurriedly to the fixed place of the ferry between Scotland and Ireland, and he was taken without hindrance until he reached the coast of Ireland. You would think each individual of the noble families of Ireland had received a kingship or a lordship when they heard that Cearbhall had come.

42] As for the king of Scotland, he decided to put Cearbhall to death on the morning of the next day. He sent the executioners for him. The prison was opened for them. They seized the prisoner and brought him to the high-king. The king looked at the prisoner, and he realized that it was not Cearbhall, and he said: 'Whom do you have, wretches?'

'Cearbhall,' said the youths.

'You have revealed your evil and your wickedness,' said the king. 'You have Fearbhlaidh.'

43] 'Truly indeed,' said the men, breaking out into smiles and laughter. The king laughed likewise and he said, 'Let the girl be released.' He forgave her for what she had done, and he thanked her for saving the poet. He sent a messenger to Ireland and he vowed that if Cearbhall should ever visit the ground of Scotland he would put him to death. He sent his twelve men after him, together with jewels and many treasures.

44] There were twelve women of the noble families of Scotland in Fearbhlaidh's retinue. Each woman had her own personal lover among Cearbhall's company. Wretched indeed, even to death, were these two bands. They treated lightly everything except the person of the other. On both sides they fell into a wasting sickness after this, so that they were three years in this strait without one of the men seeing his wife or one of the women seeing her husband. There were the usual messages, jewels, gifts and letters between them. However, of the two sides none survived by the third year except three of the women and five of the men. None of the living men had a wife who was alive among the women, nor did any of the living women have a husband who was alive among the men. It was worse for Cearbhall, however, over and above everyone, for he became a terrible churl, so that neither friend nor companion would recognize his shape or his appearance.

45]   As for Donnchadh Mór and the men of Connacht likewise, they gathered in one place to see what they should do about Cearbhall. They decided to bring evil sorcerers to him who would give him drinks of forgetfulness, and this was done so that Cearbhall did not remember ever having seen Fearbhlaidh with his eyes, and he was healed from all sickness.

46]   All the Connachtmen advised him to marry. The king of Uí Mhaine, namely Conchobhair mac Ceallaigh mhic Fhiannachta, had a beautiful, marriageable daughter. That maiden surpassed the women of her time for beauty. Ailbhe was her name, and she was betrothed to Cearbhall. A great wedding-feast was held by the nobles of Connacht. These tidings were revealed to Duibhghil, and she told them to Fearbhlaidh.

47]   'Let us go to see them,' said the girl.

'Let us do so,' said Duibhghil. They went without stopping until they were in the chambers where Cearbhall and his bride would sleep. The uproar of the wedding was going on, and Fearbhlaidh recited these verses:

48] Duighbhil, do you hear the uproar
in the house outside with the great assembly?
It is not pleasant for my ear as it hears
the uproar of the wedding of Ó Dálaigh's son.

Evil my friend Cearbhall found
while I might be marriageable,
to have the uproar of a wedding in his house
in preference to my father's daughter.

My curse and God's curse,
the curse of the saints of this world,
to a woman who will believe a man's voice
after Cearbhall, oh Duibhghil.

49] She wrote these verses on the corner of Cearbhall's harp in her own blood with a small knife. After the feast was ended, Cearbhall went to his sleeping-chamber, looked at the harp, read the verses and remembered Fearbhlaidh. The signs of death came upon him so that his appearance and his senses were deranged, and he recited this poem:

50] Red tonight is the corner of my harp;
beloved is the blood which is on it:
Beloved is the hand and beloved is the blood,
the love for which is grievously wounding me.

Beloved is the hand, indeed, beloved is the hand,
which wrote that cross in the surface.
Beloved is the hand which wrote the cross
with a small knife and with a white palm.

Beloved is the little knife with an ivory luster
of which the ivory was carved with gold-craft.
Beloved is the curly, round-ringed hair,
beloved are the palm and red mouth.

51] After that, Cearbhall began to play his harp
until dawn, and to recite these verses with it,
without stopping or ceasing, and Ó Ceallaigh's
daughter alone in the chamber until the morning
of the next day.
52] Ailbhe arose early in the morning and com-
plained about Cearbhall to all his friends. They
went to speak with Cearbhall and they asked him
what was the delusion or deception which had
overcome him. He did not answer them as
though he could not hear anything they said.
However, he began to play his harp and sing the
verses as he had before, until his companions
seized his harp from his hands by force.
Nevertheless, Cearbhall did not speak to them,
and he did not look at any of them. A full fortnight

the nobles were remaining before him in the hope that sense would come to him.

53] That was pointless for them. His case grew worse each day so that they finally had to take leave of one another and go to their own houses in each direction. They left him in Aughrim of Uí Mhaine without sense or speech.

54] However, Fearbhlaidh and Duibhghil used to be with him at night. Everyone heard that and a guard was set for them in the hope that they would be taken. That was revealed to the women and they left the house he was in. He used to come to meet the women on the shore of the Suck each day. The women used to come as two bright swans to meet him. One day Ó Ceallaigh's herdsman was at the stream before Cearbhall. He saw the two bright swans on the shore. He took stones from the bank of the strand and threw them so that he hit one of the swans and broke her wing, so that she fell on the shore. That was when Cearbhall reached them. He raised up the swan and wept bitterly above her, and recited these verses:

55] Cowherd of Aughrim,
     what came to your attention
     so that you killed my swan
     among the swans of the place?

I did not have chattel
except two beautiful, young swans.
Though their movement was quick,
they were better than one hundred herds
of cattle.

You made an unseemly cast
at one of the two noble, white swans.
It afflicted my five senses;
my curse on you, cowherd.

56]   After that, Cearbhall plunged his sword
into the herdsman so that he split his heart in
two, and he was dead and without life. The other
swan came to earth after that, and then they
resumed their own shapes. Duibhghil's left arm
was broken. Cearbhall greatly lamented that, and
very great sorrow seized him, and he recited
these verses:

57] Alas your hand, Duibhghil,
    it is the banishment of health and a
    mental derangement.
    The alteration of your form was a crime;
    the soft hand was more pleasing around you.

    Alas, the hand which was a pillow of high-kings
    was injured on both sides.
    The pang did not strike before the weapon point;
    my heart was pierced in my gnawing pain.

Everyone's anguish is not surprising
over that palm being as it is.
It was a story to rake up women's sorrow;
it was a mental derangement for heroes.

If it be heard from me, Duibhghil,
that your hand is in shreds as it is,
many are the eyebrows which would be wet,
woven with tears
and mournful because of it in Ireland.

Many are the royal sons of the kings
of Ireland,
many the warriors and many the youths
to whom the ruin of the hand and the sorrow
which has happened to you is an anguish.

Many are the pure-minded poets
and many the gentle, virginal maidens
to whom what was done to you is a grief,
oh langorous, bright-shining, brilliant one.

The warriors of Scotland grieve,
woe to me who received the reproach.
The wounding of the hand went through me;
I am ashamed to count you as nothing.

I am sorry for your sake;
'I grieve,' says Fearbhlaidh herself.
Your hand is powerless today,
beloved one of the shining kings of the Gaels.

[72]

Within my memory I do not recall
that any woman in Ireland had a hand
which was more peaceful than that one,
oh branch of the true apple-tree from Scotland.

The gentle hand by which jewels were bestowed
was often seen over the window-sill,
filling the soft, smooth, fine satin sleeve
of the gold and silver border.

Often there was another feat,
the capturing of gilded chessmen.
So that hand is a torment to me,
the hand defending upon the chessboard.

Since I saw the form of the hand
my mind is lifeless.
I am not ashamed of my weeping;
my mind is not under control.

So great is your misery
that I do not enjoy the sound of harps or
listening to poetry,
the outcry of organs or the speech of women,
or the discourse of people on the earth.

The point of my sight was distorted;
I do not see the firmament.
The news merits my putting off my form;
it has wounded me, I shall not live tomorrow.

58] They decided to make a magical ship at once, and Fearbhlaidh and Duibhghil went into it. They went until they were on their own sun-roof in the place of the king of Scotland. The news that Duibhghil had been wounded in the hand was heard in the whole court, and she was a full year recovering. Some time after that, the king heard that Fearbhlaidh was often coming to Cearbhall in those shapes, so that he devised an accursed plot to cause the destruction of Cearbhall and Fearbhlaidh.

59] One day the king was out on the castle wall so that he saw two Irishmen coming towards him. He came to them and asked them for news and where they were from. 'From Ireland,' they said.

'You will have a good reward if you do something for me,' he said.

'What is that?' they asked.

'Tell my daughter that Cearbhall Ó Dálaigh has died.'

'We shall do that,' they said.

60] They went into the fortress then, and they told their news and the events of each day consecutively since they had left Cruachan of Connacht. 'Do you have news from Ireland?' everyone asked.

'Important news,' they said. 'Cearbhall Ó Dálaigh has died from a mysterious wasting sickness, and the men of Connacht are afflicted with grief for him.'

61] As soon as Fearbhlaidh heard that, her soul

leaped from her mouth and she fell prostrate on the chessboard which was before her. Everyone rushed to save her, but they found her lifeless. The king came to her, and he began to speak to her with words of kindness, to raise her into a sitting position, to bend her limbs, to kiss her, to threaten and cajole her alternately. But he was no better off, and he had to bury the girl. Her funeral rites were performed, and her tombstone raised above her grave, and her name was written in ogham as was customary.

62] The king was indeed sorrowful, and he proclaimed that he would hang the two Irishmen for his daughter's death. 'Let it not be done,' said the men, 'for what you say is not the truth of a prince. We did nothing except what you asked us to do, and for that reason you will have from us what you judge to be fair.'

'Your word to that,' said the king.

'You will have it,' each said.

'Go to Ireland,' he said, 'and tell Cearbhall of Fearbhlaidh's death so that he will die from grief for her. By my word verily,' said the king, 'unless you do that, for all eternity I shall not catch an Irishman whom I shall not put to death.'

63] The youths did as the king said to them. One day Cearbhall was in his father's house when he saw the two strangers coming towards him. He asked them for news. They said what they had been bound to say, that Fearbhlaidh had died and how she had died. When Cearbhall heard that, he laid his head on the corner of his harp and died immediately. That was heard in the four corners of Connacht so that none of the Connachtmen consumed food or drink for three days and three nights after that. So that is the adventure and death of Cearbhall and Fearbhlaidh.

NOTES

1   Alan Bruford dates the romance to pre-1500 (*Gaelic Folktales and Medieval Romances* [Dublin, 1969], p. 42, n. 16). Proinsias Mac Cana dates it to the fifteenth or sixteenth century ('The Sinless Otherworld of *Immram Brain*,' *Ériu* 27 [1976], 105). T. F. O'Rahilly dates it as 'probably' sixteenth century ('Irish Poets, Historians and Judges in English Documents, 1538-1615,' *Proceedings of the Royal Irish Academy* 36 [1922], 102).
2   Paul Walsh, ed., 'Bas Cearbhaill and Farbhlaidhe,' *Irisleabhar Muighe Nuadhat* (1928), 26.
3   O. Bergin and R. I. Best, eds. and trans., 'Tochmarc Étaíne,' *Ériu* 12 (1938), 189.
4   'The Wooing of Etain,' in *Ancient Irish Tales*, ed. T. P. Cross and C. H. Slover (Dublin, 1969), 92.
5   T. F. O'Rahilly, *Early Irish History and Mythology* (Dublin, 1957), 6, 202; M. A. O'Brien, *Corpus Genealogiarum Hiberniae* (Dublin, 1962), 328-29.
6   Cross and Slover, 92; E. Gwynn, *The Metrical Dindshenchas* (Dublin, 1903-35), II, 2.
7   T. Ó Raithbheartaigh, *Genealogical Tracts I* (Dublin, 1932), 92.
8   O'Brien, 121.
9   C. McGrath, ed. and trans., 'Two Skilful Musicians,' *Éigse* 7 (1953), 89-90. The MS has the contraction *Fg* for the name of Baillgheal's abductor, which McGrath expands to *Fearghus*, although it seems more likely to be *Forgna* given the genealogical tradition, as I have indicated.
10 A. G. van Hamel, ed., 'Tochmarc Emire,' in *Compert Con Culainn and Other Stories* (Dublin, 1968), 62-65; 'The Wooing of Emer,' in Cross and Slover, 169-71.
11 C. Marstrander, ed. and trans., 'The Deaths of Lugaid and Derbforgaill,' *Ériu* 5 (1912), 208, 214; M. Dillon, ed., *Serglige Con Culainn* (Dublin, 1953), 2-3; 'The Sick-Bed of Cu Chulainn,' in Cross and Slover, 179.
12 Marstrander, 208, 214.
13 W. Meid, ed., *Táin Bó Fraích* (Dublin, 1967), 1.
14 D. A. Binchy, ed., *Scéla Cano Meic Gartnáin* (Dublin, 1963), 2.
15 Binchy, 7.
16 P. MacCana, 'Aspects of the Theme of King and Goddess in Irish Literature', *Études Celtiques* 7 (1955), 76-114. See also T. F. O'Rahilly, 'Éagmhais, éagmais,' *Ériu* 13 (1942), 188-90, and M. A. O'Brien, 'Grád écmaise,' *Celtica* 3 (1956), 179.

17   H. Waddell, *The Wandering Scholars* (London, 1958), 227, citing A. Jeanroy, ed., *Chansons de Jaufre Rudel* (Paris, 1924), 21.
18   F. Shaw, ed., *Aislinge Óenguso* (Dublin, 1934); K. Jackson, trans., 'The Dream of Oenghus,' in *A Celtic Miscellany* (Harmondsworth, 1971), 93-96; G. and T. Jones, trans., 'The Dream of Macsen Wledig,' in *The Mabinogion* (London, 1970), 79-88.

19   M. MacCraith, 'Ní hadhbhar seargtha go seirc,' Sixth International Congress of Celtic Studies, Galway, 9 July 1979.
20   MacCana, 'The Sinless Otherworld,' 105.
21   Bergin and Best, 180-81.
22   Binchy, 11.
23   Nessa Ní Shéaghdha, ed. and trans., *Tóruigheacht Dhiarmada agus Ghráinne* (Dublin, 1967), 10-15.
24   'The Second Battle of Mag Tured,' in Cross and Slover, 47; Elizabeth Gray, '*Mag Tuired:* The Structure of Myth in Irish Tradition,' Diss. Harvard 1974, 247-48.
25   Meid, 405; J. Carney, 'Composition and Structure of *TBF,*' in *Studies in Irish Literature and History* (Dublin, 1955), 4.
26   Meid, 2-3; Carney, 2.
27   Meid,5; Carney, 5.
28   Meid, 2; Carney, 2.
29   Carney, 'The Irish Elements in *Beowulf,*' in *Studies,* 82-83.
30   Meid, 32-33.
31   G and T. Jones, 'Peredur son of Efrawg,' in *The Mabinogion,* 199; V. Hull, ed. and trans., *Longes mac nUislenn* (New York, 1949), 62-63.
32   Georges Dumézil, *L'idéologie tripartie des Indo-Européens* (Brussels, 1958), 26. My thanks to Tomás Ó Cathasaigh for this reference.
33   from Eg. 1782, E. Windisch, ed., 'Tochmarc Étaíne,' in *Irische Texte* 1 (1880), 119. Cross and Slover, 83.
34   E. Knott, ed., *Togail Bruidne Da Derga* (Dublin, 1963), 2.
35   C. O'Rahilly, ed. and trans., *Táin Bó Cúalnge from the Book of Leinster* (Dublin, 1967), 5; 143.
36   M. Dillon, ed. and trans., *Serglige Con Culainn* (Columbus, Ohio, 1941), 27-28; 48.
37   W. W. Comfort, trans., 'Yvain,' in *Chrétien de Troyes, Arthurian Romances* (London, 1970), 216.
38   Alan S. Fedrick, trans., *The Romance of Tristan and the Tale of Tristan's Madness* (Harmondsworth, 1970), 163.
39   MacCana, 'The Sinless Otherworld,' 105.
40   Bruford, *Gaelic Folktales,* 26.

[78]

41　'The Exile of the Sons of Usnech,' in Cross and Slover, 239-47; T. Kinsella, trans., 'Exile of the sons of Uisliu,' in *The Tain* (Oxford, 1970), 8-20.

42　Fedrick, 163-64.

43　Walsh, 27.

44　J. O'Donovan, *The Tribes and Customs of Hy-Many* (Dublin, 1843), 100-05.

45　J. O'Donovan, ed. and trans., *Annals of the Kingdom of Ireland by the Four Masters* (Dublin, 1848-51),III, 309.

46　J. O'Donovan, *The Tribes of Ireland: A Satire, by Aenghus O'Daly* (1852: rpt. Cork, 1976), 8.

47　T. D. Robinson, *The Burren: A Map of the Uplands of Northwest Clare* (Cill Ronain, 1977).

48　RIA 24D 6, 37.

49　O'Donovan, *Tribes of Ireland*, 9.

50　D. Ó hÓgáin, 'Friotal na hÉigse, i.e., Staidéar ar ósnádúrthacht na filíochta i gCultúr na hÉireann,' Diss. University College, Dublin, 1977, 330.

51　cited in Ó hÓgáin, 337.

52　J. Walker, *Historical Memoirs of the Irish Bards* (London, 1786), I, 281.

53　O'Rahilly, 'Irish Poets,' 102.

54　G. Cuningham, *Burren Journey* (Limerick, 1978), 44.

55　O'Donovan, *Tribes and Customs*, 103.

56　O'Donovan, *Tribes of Ireland*, 8.

57　W. J. Watson, *The Celtic Place-Names of Scotland* (Edinburgh, 1926), 395.

58　Watson, 395.

59　A. G. van Hamel, ed., 'Aided Oenfir Aife,' in *Compert Con Culainn*, 15; T. Kinsella, trans., 'The Death of Aife's One Son,' in *The Tain*, 45.

60　Comfort, 270; Mario Roques, ed., *Le Chevalier de la Charrete* (Paris, 1967), p. 2, line 28.

61　Bruford, 35.

62　O'Donovan, *Tribes and Customs*, 104.

63　*Ériu* 4 (1910), 62-63.

64　Walsh, 27.

65　P. Mac Aogáin, ed., *Graiméir Ghaeilge na mBráthar Míonúr* (Dublin, 1968), 140.

66　'Tuireamh Philip meic Aodha Uí Raghallaigh,' in J. Carney, ed., *Poems on the O'Reillys* (Dublin, 1950), 143, line 3291.

67　'Cú Mairghréige,' in L. McKenna, ed. and trans., *Áithdioghluim Dána* (Dublin, 1939), I, 181; II, 106.

68 'Ailí Ní Chearbhaill,' in B. Ó Buachalla, ed., *Nua-dhuanaire* (Dublin, 1976), II, 15.

69 'Mo chreach is mo léan ó fhearta Dé,' in S. Mag Uidhir, ed., *Pádraig Mac a Liondain: Dánta* (Dublin, 1977), 17-18.

70 in Br. Lib. Add. 40766, fol. 58-58b, and TCD H.5.3, p.100. An edition and translation of this poem are included in my dissertation, 'Cearbhall Ó Dálaigh: An Irish Poet in Romance and Oral Tradition,' Harvard 1981, 112-15.

71 in TCD H.3.23, pp. 297-312 (1718), and Br. Lib. Eg. 170, fols. 44-52 (1724). An edition and translation of this redaction are also included in my dissertation, pp. 119-44.

72 Gilbert 136, Dublin City Library.

73 Sir Walter Scott, *Minstrelsy of the Scottish Border* (Kelso, 1802), II, 15.

74 RIA 24 D 6; a later copy is in RIA 24 D 15.

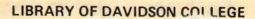